# The Kid and the Chameleon Go to School

# Also by Sheri Mabry

The Kid and the Chameleon
The Kid and the Chameleon Sleepover

# The Kid and the Chameleon Go to School

Sheri Mabry

**illustrated by**
Joanie Stone

Albert Whitman & Company
Chicago, Illinois

To: all whom I've had the honor to teach.
And all whom I've been honored to learn from,
including my family. I'm grateful. For: my favorite
classroom-the woods and the wild.—SM

To John and Yvette—JS

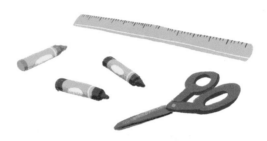

Library of Congress Cataloging-in-Publication data is on file with the publisher.

Text copyright © 2019 by Sheri Mabry
Illustrations copyright © 2019 by Albert Whitman & Company
Illustrations by Joanie Stone
First published in the United States of America
in 2019 by Albert Whitman & Company
ISBN 978-0-8075-4177-7 (hardcover)
ISBN 978-0-8075-4165-4 (ebook)

Printed in China
10 9 8 7 6 5 4 3 2 1 WKT 24 23 22 21 20 19

Design by Morgan Beck

For more information about Albert Whitman & Company,
visit our website at www.albertwhitman.com.

100 Years of Albert Whitman & Company
Celebrate with us in 2019!

# Chapter One

A chameleon sat on a leaf.

He looked down. He saw a kid.

A kid skipped past a tree.

She looked up. She saw a chameleon.

"Newton! I've been looking everywhere for you!" said the kid.

"You didn't need to look everywhere, Tessy," said the chameleon. "Just here."

"Where are you going?" asked Newton.

"To school," said Tessy. "I don't want to be late."

"What's school?" asked Newton.

"School is a place where you learn things," said Tessy. "Like math and reading and art."

"It does not sound like a chameleon thing."

"It's mostly a kid thing," said Tessy. "But you can come. We will learn new things *together*!"

"You're a kid. I'm a chameleon," said Newton. "I'm not making any promises."

# Chapter Two

Tessy showed Newton her classroom.

"Welcome to school! This is my cubby. It's where I put my backpack. This is my desk," said Tessy. "It's where I do work. See, my name is on it."

Newton crawled into the desk.

"My name is not on it," he said.

"It's where I won't do work. I'll nap instead."

A woman stood near the board. "Hello class! Please take out your crayons and draw a picture of something in this room."

"Who is *that*?" asked Newton. "And why is she telling you what to do?"

"Shh," said Tessy. "She's the teacher. That's her job."

Tessy took out her crayons. She put Newton on her desk.

"*You* are something in this room. I'm going to draw *you*," she said.

"Will it hurt?" asked Newton.

"No," said Tessy. "But hold still."

"That will not be a problem," said Newton.

Newton sat still. He turned brown.

Tessy got out the brown crayon. She began to draw.

Newton changed colors. He turned green.

Tessy sighed. She got out the green crayon. She began to draw again.

Newton changed colors.

"Newton!" said Tessy, "Stop changing colors!"

"Now *you* are bossy!" said Newton. "I don't think I like school."

He turned brown again.

"When can we go outside?" asked Newton.

Tessy shook her head. "Not now. It's time for art."

"What is art?" asked Newton.

"It's where we learn about colors," said Tessy. "You'll see."

"I already know about colors," mumbled Newton.

"Class, today we are going to paint a rainbow," said the teacher. "Please mix a little bit of blue paint, and a little bit of yellow paint. What do you get?"

Tessy mixed the colors.

"Green!" she said.

Newton yawned.

"Mix a little bit of blue paint and a little bit of red paint. What do you get?" asked the teacher.

"Purple!" said Tessy.

Newton yawned again.

"Now mix a little bit of red paint and a little bit of yellow paint. What do you get?" asked the teacher.

"That's it!" said Newton. "This school is not for me!"

"Newton, it's important to learn about colors! We can make a rainbow with paint!" said Tessy.

"I don't need paint," said Newton. He began to turn colors.

"You *do* look like a rainbow!" said Tessy.

"I told you I know about colors," said Newton. "More to the point, I *showed* you I know about colors."

Just then, the teacher walked over.

"Tessy? Who are you talking to?" she asked.

Tessy's face turned red.

"Looks like you're getting the hang of colors too, Tessy," whispered Newton.

Tessy's face turned redder.

# Chapter Three

The teacher handed out papers.

"Class, it's time for math. Please find your ruler," she said.

"*Ruler*?" said Newton. "I don't follow any rules except chameleon rules!"

Newton curled his tail around his head.

Tessy laughed. "Newton, the teacher wants us to take out *this*. It is called a ruler. It tells you how long something is. Come here. I'll measure you!"

"Will it hurt?" asked Newton.

"No, but hold still," said Tessy.

"That won't be a problem," said Newton.

"You are seven inches long!" said Tessy.

"Is that bad?" asked Newton.

"No, it's not bad," said Tessy.

"Is it good?" asked Newton.

"It's not good either," said Tessy. "It just is."

"I don't see the point of math," said Newton. "If all you are doing is finding out what already is."

"Can we go outside now?" asked Newton.

"Not now," said Tessy. "Look at the clock. It is snack time and rest time!"

"Hmn. Snacks and rest," said Newton. "Maybe I like school after all."

"And we might have a spelling bee," said Tessy.

"They're not my favorite," said Newton. "Too sweet and sticky."

"Not a bumblebee. A spelling bee. Where we learn to spell."

"I like the snack and rest time," said Newton. "It's more a chameleon thing."

Tessy waited for the crackers to be handed out.

She waited for the juice box.

She looked for Newton.

She could not find him.

Tessy looked under her desk.

Newton wasn't there.

Tessy looked in her desk.

Newton wasn't there either.

Tessy looked in the animal area.

"Newton, what are you doing over *here*?" she asked. "The snacks are over *there*!"

"There are snacks over *here* too," said Newton.

He flicked his tongue. He swallowed.

"Mnn. That hit the spot. Flies are so much better than bees."

Newton closed one eye. Then the other.

"But I brought you a graham cracker," said Tessy. "They are my very favorite snack!"

Newton opened one eye.

"I'll take that one," said Newton.

"The bigger one?" said Tessy. "Are you sure?"

"Yes, it's perfect!" said Newton.

"It sure is perfect," said Tessy. She slowly handed him the bigger cracker.

"I thought you already had a snack," said Tessy. She began eating the smaller cracker.

"I did," said Newton. "I want to try measuring."

"I could measure it for you," said Tessy.

"No, like I said, I'm not fond of rulers," said Newton. "I'll measure it chameleon style."

Newton flicked his tongue.

"Yep," he said. He crawled onto the cracker. He stretched out.

"Chameleon length. The perfect place to nap."

He closed one eye, then the other. He fell asleep.

# Chapter Four

"It's time to read, Newton," said Tessy. "Here is a book."

"No books," said Newton. "I read chameleon style. As I already told you, this school is not for me! I'm going outside!"

Tessy put her hands on her hips.

"Newton, you don't want to read, or paint, or do math! All you want to do is go outside!" said Tessy.

The bell rang. Newton went outside. Tessy followed.

"Why did you want to go outside? Is it so you can find bugs to eat?" asked Tessy. She crossed her arms.

"No," said Newton.

"Is it so you can find trees to climb?" asked Tessy. She stomped her foot.

"No," said Newton.

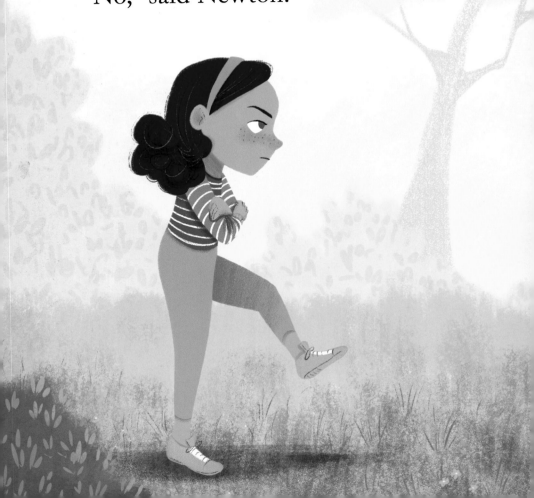

"It is so you can find rocks to nap on?" asked Tessy. She squeezed her eyebrows together.

"No," said Newton.

"I wanted to go outside to show you chameleon school," said Newton. Tessy looked at Newton. He was gazing up at the sky.

"I don't read books," said Newton.
"I read clouds. The sky says it is going
to rain soon."

Tessy uncrossed her arms.

Newton flicked his tongue. He flicked it again.

"I don't measure with a ruler," said Newton. "I measure with my tongue. The wind says the storm is coming fast."

Tessy raised her eyebrows.

"I tell time by where the sun is," said
Newton. "And you already know that
I know my colors."

Tessy laughed.

"Look at the sky," said Newton.
"*Now* is the time to get under
the tree!"

Tessy reached out a hand. Newton
scrambled on.
She ran under the tree with Newton.

It started to rain.

The wind blew hard.

The clouds rolled in the sky.

All of the other kids started to yell and run inside.

But Tessy and Newton stayed dry.

"I learned something new today, Newton," said Tessy.

"What is that?" asked Newton.

"I learned that there are different places to learn," said Tessy.

"Yep, there sure are," said Newton. "You're a kid. I'm a chameleon."

"I learned something new today too, Tessy," said Newton.

"What is that?" asked Tessy.

"Graham crackers make a nice napping spot. Especially when a friend gives you her favorite, biggest one."

Tessy's cheeks turned pink.
Newton turned yellow. And red.
"Newton!" said Tessy. "Yellow and red make orange!"
"They sure do," said Newton.

The sun peeked out from behind a cloud.

It lit up the falling raindrops.

"Look!" said Tessy.

"I see," said Newton.

Tessy and Newton sat under the tree, watching the rainbow…*together.*

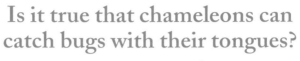

# Chameleon Facts

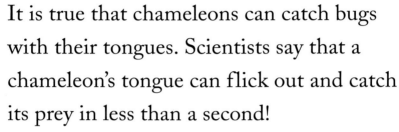

### Is it true that chameleons can catch bugs with their tongues?

It is true that chameleons can catch bugs with their tongues. Scientists say that a chameleon's tongue can flick out and catch its prey in less than a second!

Some chameleons can shoot their tongues out to twice the length of their body! The tongue forms a suction cup when it hits its target. Then, ta-da! Dinner!